a	we	on	do	go	out
I	and	run	did	up	look
is	can	not	get	for	funny
in	see	be	like	to	come
it	you	no	make	down	jump
me	the	say	are	here	was

*More words at the back of the book!

**To our agent, Bri, for finding our little books a home.
And to our editor, Tamar, for nurturing them along until they
were ready to be kicked back out into the world again.
—K.B. & B.H.**

One of the first and most important steps to becoming a reader is mastering basic sight words. These "sight words" are the most frequently used words in the English language, the basic building blocks and connectors in every text children will encounter. So fluent readers need to recognize and read them automatically "on sight."

This book is designed to teach 59 of the very first of those sight words.

Kevin Bolger
Reading Specialist

Library of Congress Control Number: 2016936184
ISBN 978-0-06-228602-4

Typography by Erica De Chavez
17 18 19 20 21 PC 10 9 8 7 6 5 4 3 2 ❖ First Edition

SEE FRED RUN

by Kevin Bolger   illustrated by Ben Hodson

HARPER

An Imprint of HarperCollinsPublishers

This is Ed.

This is Ed on a bike.

That is Fred in the road.

Ed rides on the bike.

Fred walks on the road.

This is Ed in a cowboy hat.

That is Fred in a chicken suit.

Ed likes his cowboy hat.

Fred likes his chicken suit.

Jump, Ed. Jump!

Come on, Fred. Run.

Okay, be like that.

See the hungry tigers, Fred?

Hungry tigers, Fred.

See Fred run.

Run, Fred. Run!

See the angry gorillas, Fred?

Angry gorillas, Fred.

See Fred leap.

See Fred swing.

See Fred . . . fly?

See Fred—

Hey, where is Fred?

This is Fred.

(In funny underpants.)

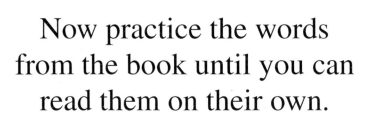

Now practice the words
from the book until you can
read them on their own.

well	going	into
will	ride	this